LET'S GO, FROGGY!

LET'S GO, FROGGY!

by JONATHAN LONDON
illustrated by FRANK REMKIEWICZ

SCHOLASTIC INC.
New York   Toronto   London   Auckland   Sydney

For Maureen and Grandma "Cook,"
who know "where it's at," and for
Sean and Aaron, who sometimes don't

With special appreciation to my
great aunt Norma Jacobson—
her joie de vivre
—J. L.

For Grace
—F.R.

ISBN 0-590-62186-6

Text copyright © 1994 by Jonathon London.
Illustrations copyright © 1994 by Frank Remkiewicz.
All rights reserved. Published by Scholastic Inc., 555 Broadway, New York, NY 10012, by arrangement with Viking Penguin, a division of Penguin Books USA Inc.

20 19 18 17   0 1 2 3 4/0

Printed in the U.S.A.   14

First Scholastic printing, March 1996

It was warm.
Froggy woke up
and looked out the window.
Birds, butterflies, flowers.
"Hurray!" sang Froggy.
"I want to go out and play!"

"Okay," said his father.
"How about a bike trip
and a picnic?
Would you like that?"

"Yes!" cried Froggy. "Let's go!"

"First you have to get ready, silly,"
said his father.

"Okay!" said Froggy. "I'm getting ready!"

So Froggy got dressed.

He pulled on his underwear—*zap!*

Pulled on his shorts—*zip!*

Pulled on his socks—*zoop!*

Pulled on his sneakers—*zup!*

And buttoned up his shirt—*zut! zut! zut!*

FRRROOGGYY!

called his father. "Let's go!"

"I'm re-e-a-d-y!" yelled Froggy and flopped out to show him—*flop flop flop.*

"But Froggy!" said his father.

"You need your bicycle helmet!"

"I don't know where it is!" said Froggy.

"It's wherever you left it!"

"I forget!"

"You have to *look* for it!"

So Froggy looked for his helmet—*flop flop flop.*

He looked under the sink—*bonk!*

He looked in the fridge—*slam!*

He looked in his toy chest.

"I found it!" yelled Froggy

and put it on with a slap—*zat!*

FRRROOGGYY!

called his father. "Let's go!"

"I'm re-e-a-d-y!" yelled Froggy—*flop flop flop.*

"You should bring your butterfly net!"
said his father.
"I don't know where it is!"
"It's wherever you left it!"

So Froggy looked for

his butterfly net—*flop flop flop.*

He looked under the coffee table—*bonk!*

He looked in the garbage can—*slam!*

He looked in his father's golf bag.

"I found it!" yelled Froggy

and swung it at a fly—*swish!*—

but missed.

FRRROOGGYY!

called his father. "Let's go!"

"I'm re-e-a-d-y!" yelled Froggy—*flop flop flop.*

"How about the ball Grandpapa gave you?"
 asked his father.
"I don't know where it is!"
"It's wherever you left it!"

So Froggy looked for his ball

—*flop flop flop.*

He looked under the stove—*bonk!*

He looked in the cookie jar—*slam!*

He looked in the bathtub.

"I found it!" he yelled

and kicked it into the goldfish bowl—*splash!*

FRRROOGGYY!

called his father. "Let's go!"

"I'm re-e-a-d-y!" yelled Froggy—*flop flop flop.*

"Let's bring the bag of peaches
   Auntie Loulou gave you," said his father.
"I don't know where it is!"
"It's wherever you left it!"

So Froggy looked for the

bag of peaches—*flop flop flop.*

He looked under the kitchen table—*bonk!*

He looked in his closet—*slam!*

He looked in his bed.

"I found it!" yelled Froggy

and took a bite—*scrunch!*

(He was getting kind of hungry.)

FRRROOGGYY!

called his father. "Let's go!"

"I'm re-e-a-d-y!" yelled Froggy—*flop flop flop.*

"Daddy, can I bring that pack of trading cards
 Uncle Gerard gave me?"
"Okay, Froggy, but hurry. Let's go!"
"I don't know where it is!"
"It's wherever you left it!"

"*Oops!* Here it is! I found it!
It was in my pocket!
Can we go now, Daddy? I'm *ready!*"

"Okay, but do you know
where my red backpack is?" asked his father.

"Daddy! *It's wherever you left it!*"

"I forget!"
Froggy pointed.

IT'S ON YOUR BACK !

Froggy laughed.
"Oops!" cried Froggy's father,
looking more red in the face than green.

Ready to go at last, Froggy flopped over
to the bicycle—*flop flop flop.*

"Let's go, Froggy!" said his father.

"I'm *hungry!*" said Froggy.

"I want to eat NOW!"

So they ate their picnic
on the patio—*munch scrunch munch.*

"Okay, I'm ready!" said Froggy.
"Let's go!" said his father.

And off they pedaled into the sunset—*wee!*